Little, Brown and Company

Hachette Book Group
1290 Avenue of the Americas, New York, NY 10104
Visit us at lb-kids.com

Little, Brown and Company is a division of Hachette Book Group, Inc.
The Little, Brown name and logo are trademarks of Hachette Book Group, Inc.

The publisher is not responsible for websites (or their content)
that are not owned by the publisher.

First Edition: October 2015

ISBN 978-0-316-37725-6

10 9 8 7 6 5 4 3 2 1

CW

Printed in the United States of America

TEEN TITANS GO!

READ AT YOUR OWN RISK

Adapted by **Magnolia Belle**

Based on the episode "**Books**"

written by **John Loy**

LITTLE, BROWN AND COMPANY
New York   Boston

The Teen Titans are hanging out at Titans Tower, and they are bored. They have defeated all their foes, watched all their TV shows, and played all their video games.

"I'm bored out of my gourd, bros!" Beast Boy declares.

"The dreary time is here for me as well," Starfire adds.

Raven is annoyed. "Do you mind? I am trying to read," she says. "Why don't you try reading a book?"

The Titans stare blankly at Raven.

"Books are worlds of imagination!" Raven continues. "They create pictures in your mind."

Beast Boy rolls his eyes. "Come on. You're just sitting there looking at words."

"Words can take you on an imagination adventure, Beast Boy!" Raven says.

Robin speaks up timidly. "Um, Raven, I'd like to go on an imagination adventure."

With a magical snap of her fingers, Raven gives the other
Titans books of their own!

"*The Return of the Invisible Man*!" Beast Boy says. He starts reading his book and howls, "My imagination is going into overdrive! Reading is fundamental, yo!"

"*The Adventures of Pinocchio!* This is so magical!" Cyborg roars.

"*The Biography of Benjamin Franklin*! This is so amazing!" Robin raves.

"*The Birdwatcher's Guide to Pelicans!*" Starfire exclaims. "My brain has never been so alive!"

The Titans are all enjoying their books, but then Robin says, "If only we could take our love of reading to the next level!"

Raven pipes up, "Well, I've always wanted to start a book club."

Cyborg is shocked. "They have clubs...for books?"

"Book clubs are for sharing comments about the books you've read!" Raven answers happily.

The Teen Titans gather around to discuss their love for their books.

Starfire hugs her pelican book and laughs. "I loved my book! The pelicans were funny. They gave me the *splinknards*!" she says.

"My book was crazy fun! It was filled with so much adventure!" Cyborg hollers. Robin gives a thumbs-up and declares, "My book had science, and science is cool!"

Raven is frustrated. "Guys! A book club is more than just sharing feelings. It's about sharing thoughts, too!"

"What's a *thought*?" Beast Boy asks.

Raven responds, "Oh, brother. For example, I found my book's premise to be unconvincing, the plot twists trite, and the philosophical underpinning a strained attempt at significance."

The other Titans gasp!

"What did you just do, Raven?" Robin inquires.

Cyborg answers angrily, "I think she just took the fun out of reading!"

The Titans are pretty bummed after Raven makes them think thoughts about their books, so Beast Boy cheers everyone up with a *song*!

"My book has a front and a back and paper in the middle.
It's got a lot of words in it—some are big; some are little!
With numbers on each page, you can't get lost.
So when I crack my book open, I read like a boss!
I love the feel of the paper, the smell of the ink.
It challenges my brain muscles; it's making me think!"

Raven, unimpressed by Beast Boy's book ballad, attempts to walk away. Robin stops her.

"Wait, Raven, we finished reading all our books—"

"And?"

"We need new books to read!" Beast Boy finishes Robin's sentence.

"So why don't you just read one another's books?" Raven recommends, then she disappears.

Without new books to read, the other Titans find themselves feeling very distraught.

Beast Boy moans. "I can feel my imagination dying! It hurts."

"There must be more books around here somewhere," Starfire suggests.

Robin commands the team to split up and find more books. "Titans, go!"

The Titans look all over the Tower for books. They try looking behind picture frames, inside the walls, under the beds, and in the dirty laundry. They even look in the toilets! There's no sign of any books.

Beast Boy's bloodhound sense of smell leads the gang to a secret treasure chest that's buried in the backyard! Cyborg pops it open with his lock-picking skills, and they find...a book!

Robin exclaims, "Let's read it!"

"Not that book. You can't read that one! That book's evil—that's why I buried it!" Raven demands.

"Too late!" Robin yells as the evil book flings open.

THE INVISIBLE MAN

PELICANS

BENJAMIN FRANKLIN

PINOCCHIO

The tome unleashes all the characters the Titans imagined from inside their heads!

"I told you not to open it!" Raven cries. "You have to turn off your imaginations to stop them."

Reading books gave the Titans such active imaginations that they're unable to stop the characters from terrorizing them!

"Reading is just too much fun, Raven!" Cyborg screams as Pinocchio gives him a thrashing.

Starfire cries, "There has to be a way to make books boring!"

Raven knows what to do. "That's it! We have to take the fun out of reading. We have to re-form the...book club!"

As the Titans are getting clobbered, they interject with thoughts about their books, which causes the imaginary characters to get sucked back into the evil book forever!

"It's over," Raven announces. The Titans all breathe a big sigh of relief. She continues, "Whaddya say we all go back to the Tower to look at comic books and eat cookies?"

"Titans, go!" Robin cheers.